KU-350-137

Tarzan ® owned by Edgar Rice Burroughs, Inc. and used by Permission.
© Edgar Rice Burroughs, Inc. and Disney Enterprises, Inc.

This is a Parragon book
This edition published in 2006

Parragon
Queen Street House
4 Queen Street
Bath, BA1 1HE, UK

Copyright © 2006 Disney Enterprises, Inc.

All rights reserved. No part of this publication may be reproduced, stored
in a retrieval system or transmitted by any means electronic, mechanical,
photocopying or otherwise without the prior permission of the publisher.

Printed in China
ISBN 1-40547-434-3

Disney
◆ PRINCESS

Storybook
Collection

p

Contents

Walt Disney's
Sleeping Beauty

Long ago, in a faraway kingdom, a tiny princess was born. Her parents, the King and Queen, named her Aurora. Her parents announced that Aurora would one day marry young Prince Phillip. He lived in a neighbouring kingdom.

To celebrate Aurora's birth, the King held a great feast at the castle. People came from near and far, bringing gifts for the child.

Three good fairies came to the feast, and they brought the baby special gifts.

"Mine shall be the gift of beauty," said the first good fairy. "Mine shall be the gift of song," said the second.

Before the third good fairy could speak, an evil witch named Maleficent appeared. She was angry because she hadn't been invited to the feast.

Maleficent warned that on Aurora's sixteenth birthday, the girl would prick her finger on a spinning wheel and die.

But the third good fairy had not yet spoken. "No, the Princess will not die!" she said quickly. "She will only sleep – until true love's kiss breaks the spell."

To keep Aurora safe, the King and Queen secretly sent her to live with the good fairies. The fairies called the child Briar Rose so that no one would know who she was.

On the day of Briar Rose's sixteenth birthday, the fairies sent her off to pick berries in the woods. Then they

began preparing for her birthday party.

The fairies had put away their magic for fear that they would be discovered by Maleficent. But after struggling with a lopsided cake and a dress that just didn't look right, they retrieved their magic wands and set about making everything perfect for Briar Rose.

Meanwhile, beautiful Briar Rose wandered through the woods with her animal friends. Suddenly a handsome young man appeared. Briar Rose did not know it was Prince Phillip.

Later that day, when the birthday celebration was over, it was time for the Princess to return to the castle. She was going to live with her parents once again.

That night the evil fairy Maleficent appeared at the castle and lured Aurora away to a lonely tower. There she tricked the Princess into touching a spinning wheel. Aurora pricked her finger

and fell into a deep sleep.

To save the King and Queen from terrible heartache, the good fairies put everyone in the castle to sleep.

Meanwhile, Maleficent wanted to keep Prince Phillip away from Aurora, so she locked the Prince in a dungeon.

Phillip was not a prisoner for long. The good fairies brought him a magic shield and sword. Soon he was on his way to rescue the Princess.

To keep Prince Phillip from entering the castle, Maleficent surrounded it with thick branches full of

thorns. But that didn't stop the Prince.

As the Prince came closer to the castle, Maleficent turned herself into an angry dragon.

It was a terrible fight, but Phillip used his magic shield

and sword and finally defeated the dragon.

Prince Phillip raced to the tower and found the sleeping

beauty. He kissed her tenderly, and the Princess awoke.

At the same moment, everyone in the castle awoke. The

King and Queen were overjoyed to see their daughter again.

Soon it was announced that Princess Aurora and Prince Phillip would marry. Everyone in the kingdom rejoiced, for they knew that Aurora and her prince would live happily ever after.

One day Pocahontas visited Grandmother Willow, a wise old tree spirit. Pocahontas was confused. Her father wanted her to marry Kocoum, a brave warrior. But Pocahontas did not believe that this was the right path for her. She had dreamed of a spinning arrow and asked Grandmother Willow about the meaning of her dream.

"It is pointing you down your path," she told Pocahontas.

"But how do I find my path?" Pocahontas asked.

"Listen with your heart and you will understand," Grandmother Willow told her. "The spirits are everywhere. They will guide you."

So Pocahontas climbed a tall tree to listen to the wind. Off in the distance she saw strange, billowing clouds.

The clouds Pocahontas thought she saw were really the sails of a large ship. Aboard were men from England coming to the New World in search of gold.

When the ship touched shore, a man called John Smith set out to explore the new land. He met a funny raccoon called Meeko, Pocahontas's friend.

Pocahontas hid from the stranger. But when he heard rustling in the bushes, he knew someone was there. Finally the two stood face-to-face. Pocahontas

was scared; she ran to her canoe to get away. But the stranger called after her. "Don't go! I won't hurt you!"

Pocahontas did not understand what John Smith was saying, but she remembered Grandmother Willow's words. When she listened with her heart, she saw that he was kind. The two quickly became friends.

Meanwhile, at Governor Ratcliffe's orders, John Smith's crew began digging up the new land in search of gold. When the Indians from Pocahontas's tribe approached the settlers, the Governor called them

"savages". He ordered his men to draw their guns and fire.

The Indians had never seen weapons like guns before. Powhatan, who was the chief and Pocahontas's father, declared war against these dangerous men.

Back in the forest, Pocahontas and John Smith got acquainted. Ever curious, and always in search of food, Meeko took a compass from John Smith's bag. "What is that?" Pocahontas asked.

"It helps you find your way when you are lost," John Smith explained. "Meeko can keep it. I can buy another one in London."

Pocahontas wanted to hear all about London. John

Smith described the wonders of the city. Then he told Pocahontas that the settlers would build a city like London in the New World. Pocahontas didn't think they needed a city in the middle of her beautiful forest. She decided it was time to introduce John Smith to the wonders of nature all around them.

Pocahontas even took John Smith to meet Grandmother Willow. He was amazed. "One look at this place and the men will forget about digging for gold," Smith said.

"What is gold?" Pocahontas asked.

John Smith showed her a gold coin. Pocahontas told him that there was nothing like this on her land.

John Smith rushed back to his camp to tell Ratcliffe that there was no gold to be found. But the Governor didn't believe him. He thought the Indians wanted to keep it all. And Ratcliffe wanted to take it by force.

When Pocahontas tried to tell her father that they must find a peaceful way to deal with the strangers, Powhatan's braves didn't agree. They wanted to fight. Pocahontas convinced her father that if one of the strangers would come and talk in peace, he must listen.

That night, Pocahontas met John Smith at Grandmother Willow. She convinced him to come with her and talk to her father. But neither she nor John Smith knew that a settler named Thomas was watching them. So was Kocoum. Suddenly Kocoum jumped out of the woods and attacked John Smith. Thomas fired at Kocoum.

"Thomas, run!" Smith cried.

As Thomas fled,

warriors captured Smith.

"At sunrise, this man will die," the chief told his people.

Pocahontas did not know what to do. Suddenly Meeko dropped the compass into her lap. She looked at the needle moving back and

forth. "The spinning arrow!" she whispered.

"It's the arrow from your dream showing you your path. Let the spirits guide you," Grandmother Willow said.

Pocahontas ran like the wind. She stopped the

warriors from hurting Smith. The Indians put down their weapons and refused to fight.

But Ratcliffe grabbed a musket and shot at Powhatan. John Smith jumped in front of the chief and took the bullet himself.

The wounded Smith had to return to England. So did the greedy governor, who was now in chains.

As they were about to set sail, Pocahontas and her friend said good-bye. "Come with me?" John Smith asked hopefully.

"I am needed here," Pocahontas replied sadly.

"Then know that wherever I am, I'll always be with you." John Smith smiled as he left.

Pocahontas knew that in their hearts, they would always be together.

WALT DISNEP'S

Snow White
and the Seven Dwarfs

Long ago, in a faraway place, there lived a lovely princess named Snow White. Her hair was black as coal, her lips red as rose and her skin as white as snow.

Snow White's stepmother, the Queen, was very cruel.

She hated anyone who was more beautiful than she. The Queen treated Snow White like a servant.

Snow White never complained. She was obedient and hard-working, but she dreamed of a handsome prince who would take her away to his castle. One day, while drawing water from the well, a handsome stranger did appear, charmed by Snow White's singing. But Snow

White was too shy to speak to him.

Inside the castle, the Queen asked her magic mirror, "Mirror, mirror, on the wall, who is the fairest one of all?"

Every day the mirror had the same reply. "You are the fairest," he told her. And the Queen was content for another day.

But as Snow White grew older, she also grew more

beautiful. And the Queen became very jealous.

One day the magic mirror told the Queen that someone else was the fairest in the land. It was the princess, Snow White!

In a jealous rage, the Queen called her royal huntsman into the throne room.

"Take Snow White far into the forest and kill her," she commanded. "And as proof of your deed, bring

me back her heart in this." She handed the stunned huntsman a beautiful carved box.

"Poor Snow White," said the hunter to the innocent

princess. "I cannot kill you. You must run away and hide from the Queen!"

Snow White was so frightened that she ran off through the dark woods.

At last she came to a cottage. "Who lives here?" Snow White wondered.

Then she heard voices singing in the distance. The seven dwarfs who lived in the cottage were coming home from a hard day at work in the diamond mine.

The dwarfs introduced themselves. Their names were Sleepy, Grumpy, Happy, Doc, Dopey, Sneezy and Bashful.

They invited Snow White to share their supper.

Snow White felt so safe with the dwarfs that she decided to stay with them.

But the evil Queen soon found out that Snow White was still alive. She would have to take matters into her own wicked hands.

She fled to the dungeon beneath the castle. There the Queen mixed a potion that would change her into an old hag. Then she took an apple and slowly dipped it into another potion. "One bite of this poisoned apple and Snow White will close her eyes

forever!" she cackled.

The old woman appeared at Snow White's window. "Hello, dearie," she said. "Taste one of my delicious apples. It's apple pies that make menfolk's mouths water. Pies made from apples like these." Then she held the

poisoned apple out to

Snow White.

The birds tried to

warn Snow White

away from the

poisoned fruit. They

fluttered and flew around the hag, trying to make her

drop the apple.

"Stop it! Stop it!" cried Snow White.

The birds flew away sadly. Then the animals of the

forest ran to the dwarfs to warn them that something was

very wrong and they needed to come right home!

The seven dwarfs raced to the cottage and found the old woman trying to sneak away and Snow White lying lifeless on the floor. The dwarfs chased the hag into the forest.

A storm began to blow as the evil woman ran away. Suddenly she came to the edge of a steep and rocky cliff.

First, she tried to move a huge rock so it would roll down on top of the poor dwarfs and crush them.

"Look out!" cried Grumpy to the others.

At that moment, lightning struck. The Queen lost her balance and fell to her doom!

The sad little dwarfs built a bed of gold and glass for their beloved Snow White. They kept watch over her, day and night.

Then one day a handsome prince rode into the forest. How beautiful the young woman was! The Prince knelt down and kissed Snow White tenderly.

His kiss awakened her. Then Snow White and the Prince rode off to his kingdom, where they lived happily ever after.

Disney's

Aladdin

THE PRINCESS
WHO DIDN'T WANT TO MARRY

Princess Jasmine giggled with her friend Rajah. Although Rajah was a tiger he had always been her closest friend. Now he held a piece of Prince Achmed's trousers in his mouth. He and Jasmine were both glad to be rid of the selfish suitor.

Jasmine's father, however, was not amused. "The law says you must be married to a prince by your next birthday."

Jasmine thought the law was unfair. She wanted to

marry for love. "Try to understand, I've never done a thing on my own," she explained. Lately she wished that she were not a princess at all. She felt as trapped as the caged doves.

That night the princess disguised herself, planning

to escape. As she began to climb over the palace wall, Rajah tugged on her dress. He was sad to see Jasmine leave, but knew what was best for her. "I can't stay here and have my life lived for me," she explained sorrowfully.

In the marketplace, life was busy and exciting. With compassion,

Jasmine handed an apple to a poor child. However, when

she was unable to pay, the vendor grabbed her angrily.

Luckily, a handsome stranger came to her rescue.

Running swiftly, they escaped to his rooftop home.

Jasmine was thrilled with the thought of such freedom. This young man had no one to tell him what he could or couldn't do. As she was imagining his carefree life, the man looked longingly towards the palace. It would be

wonderful to live there, he thought, without having to worry about where to find his next meal.

"Sometimes I just feel so trapped," they both expressed at the same time.

Surprised, they looked at each other. Feeling a deep bond with this handsome stranger, Jasmine leaned to kiss

him, when suddenly guards burst upon them. There was nowhere to escape.

"Do you trust me?" asked the young man, holding out his hand to her. She looked into his brown eyes and placed her fingers in his grip. Quickly, they jumped off the tall building, their fall broken by a pile of hay. "I've got you

this time, Street Rat!"
yelled another guard.
Jasmine revealed herself
as a princess but they still
arrested her friend. "My
orders come from Jafar,"
the guard told her.

Back at the palace,
Jasmine confronted her
father's chief adviser. The
evil Jafar cruelly deceived
her into thinking that her

handsome stranger was dead. "Oh, Rajah," she wept, as the tiger tried to comfort her.

Many days later, on the streets of Agrabah, there was a magnificent parade. Princess Jasmine, still grieving,

watched from her balcony. Trumpets were blaring, animals were doing tricks, fireworks blasted, but most impressive was Prince Ali, sitting on top of an enormous elephant, throwing gold coins into the crowd. Jasmine shook her head in disgust. Did he think he could buy her hand in marriage?

With anger, she yelled at the prince, "I am not a prize to be won!" But Prince Ali would not give up. That evening he appeared on her balcony. Rajah growled

protectively and was about to chase him away but

Jasmine thought he looked familiar. She stepped closer

and he showed her his magic carpet. "We could get out of

the palace . . . see

the world," Prince

Ali offered.

Jasmine

hesitated until he

leaned forward

offering his hand.

"Do you trust

me?" he asked, and immediately Jasmine knew this was the same stranger she had met in the marketplace. Eagerly she climbed aboard and the carpet took them into the star-filled sky. Never had she seen such wonders! As they flew, she felt happier than she ever had before. Leaning on Prince Ali's shoulder she held his hand, not wanting the romantic night to end.

Unfortunately, Jafar soon discovered Prince Ali's magic lamp. He revealed Jasmine's love to be Aladdin, a poor boy from Agrabah. He had used a wish from the

genie in the lamp to transform himself into Prince Ali.

"Jasmine, I'm sorry I lied to you about being a prince," said Aladdin humbly. Jasmine held his

hands. She didn't love him for being a prince. She loved him for himself. Even the Sultan realized that Aladdin was worthy. When her father changed the law to allow his daughter to marry the man of her choice, Jasmine said, "I choose Aladdin." As fireworks lit the sky and the Genie and Abu waved goodbye, Aladdin and Jasmine shared a kiss on their magic carpet. Beneath them was a whole new

world where they would live together, happily ever after.

Disney's

Beauty
AND
THE
BEAST

Once upon a time there was a prince who was so selfish and unkind that he and all who lived in his castle were put under a powerful spell.

The prince was turned into a terrible beast. He would

change back into a prince only if he learned to love

someone and be loved in return.

In a nearby village lived a beautiful young woman

named Belle. She loved to read books about adventure

and romance.

Gaston, the hunter, followed Belle everywhere in town. He wanted to marry her, but Belle thought Gaston was a conceited bully.

One dark winter day, Belle's father, Maurice, started off on a journey through the woods and lost his way. Maurice found shelter in a gloomy castle. There he was greeted by the Beast's servants. The spell had changed them all into enchanted objects.

Before long Maurice was discovered by the Beast!

"What are you staring at?" roared the angry beast.

Then he threw Maurice into a dungeon.

Maurice's horse came home alone. "Where's Papa?"

cried Belle. "Take me to him!" Belle climbed on, and the

horse galloped back to the Beast's castle.

The Beast terrified Belle, but she tried to be brave.

"Let my father go!" she cried. "Let me take his place."

The Beast agreed, but only if Belle promised to stay in his gloomy castle forever.

The Beast's enchanted servants welcomed Belle and tried to make her feel at home. There was Cogsworth the

mantel clock, Lumiere the candelabra and Mrs Potts the teapot. They knew that if Belle and the Beast fell in love, the spell that lay over the castle would be broken.

Little by little the Beast grew kinder towards Belle.

One day he led her to his magnificent library.

"It's wonderful!" Belle gasped.

"It's yours," said the Beast.

Belle slowly grew fonder of the Beast and learned to

trust him. She even taught him how to dance. But her
heart ached for her father. "If only I could see him again,"
she told the Beast.

"Come with me," he answered. "I will show him to you."

The Beast's rooms showed the effects of his anger and despair. Belle held up a magic mirror and saw Maurice, looking tired and sick.

"I must go to him!" cried Belle.

The Beast agreed to let Belle go, even though it meant the end of his hopes for breaking the spell.

When Belle returned home, she told Gaston about the Beast's kindness. Gaston was jealous.

He convinced the villagers that the Beast was a monster and should be destroyed. He led the angry mob to the Beast's castle.

Gaston found the Beast and fought him on the castle rooftops. In the midst of the battle, Gaston lost his footing and fell to his death – but not before he had stabbed the Beast.

Belle rushed to the Beast's side only to find him badly wounded. "You came back," he whispered.

Belle's tears fell upon the Beast. "I love you," she cried.

The spell was broken! The Beast was transformed into a handsome prince, and the enchanted servants became human once more. Belle and her prince would live very happily ever after.

Walt Disney's

Cinderella

Once upon a time, there was a pretty young girl named Cinderella. Cinderella was loved by everyone because she was good and sweet and kind. But Cinderella's widowed father believed she needed a mother. So he married again to a woman with two

daughters of her own. Soon Cinderella's father died and she was left to live with her mean stepmother and two jealous stepsisters in the attic of their house.

Poor Cinderella had to do all of the cooking and cleaning. She no longer had nice things and wore only tattered old clothes, while her stepmother and stepsisters had very nice clothes and lived very comfortably.

But no matter how mean her stepmother

and stepsisters were, Cinderella was always cheerful. Even the little animals loved to be near her. She made friends with the mice and birds, making them little outfits to wear and caring for them. Two of Cinderella's best friends were Jaq and Gus. Cinderella and Jaq were always saving Gus from mean old Lucifer the cat, who had his eye on the plump little mouse.

One day a letter came

inviting everyone to the palace for a ball. Cinderella's stepmother said, "Cinderella may go, but only if she finishes her work." Cinderella happily washed, ironed and scrubbed the floors all day.

Meanwhile, Cinderella's little friends went to work

making her a lovely gown. The birds and mice who loved Cinderella wanted so much to surprise her. And when she saw what they had done, she was very touched. She put on the beautiful dress and ran downstairs to join her stepsisters.

The birds and mice had used sashes and ribbons and beads that belonged to Cinderella's stepsisters to make

the dress look nice. But when her stepsisters saw the

gown, they tore it to shreds.

"That's my ribbon!" cried one.

"And those are my beads!" yelled the other.

Cinderella ran to the garden in tears. "Now I can't go

to the ball!" she cried.

"Don't cry, child," said a gentle voice. "I am your fairy godmother, and I have come to help you."

Then the Fairy Godmother waved her wand. Four mice became four proud white horses, and a big, round pumpkin became a glittering coach.

Again the Fairy Godmother waved her wand and turned Cinderella's torn dress into a beautiful gown. "You must leave the ball by midnight," she warned. "After that, the magic spell will be broken."

At the ball, the Prince danced with Cinderella all evening. She felt as if she were floating on a dream!

The King and the Grand Duke were delighted to see them falling in love.

But as the clock struck midnight, Cinderella ran from the palace. She was in such a hurry that she left one glass slipper behind. The Prince ran after her, but it was too late.

The next day, the Prince sent the Grand Duke door-to-door to find the young woman who had lost her slipper. When they got to Cinderella's house, both stepsisters tried on the glass slipper, but their feet were much too big.

Cinderella's stepmother told the Grand Duke that there were no other ladies in the house. She had locked Cinderella in her room upstairs on purpose. But Cinderella's little friends Gus and Jaq stole the key from her stepmother's pocket, opened her door and freed Cinderella just in time.

When Cinderella appeared and asked if she could try on the slipper, her stepmother was furious. She tripped the footman who was holding the slipper on a pillow.

It fell to the floor and shattered.

But Cinderella reached into her apron pocket and pulled out the matching one. It was a perfect fit!

The Grand Duke was happy and relieved that he had found the slipper's owner. The Prince would be married at last. And Cinderella's dreams would all come true.

DISNEY'S
THE LITTLE MERMAID

PRINCESS OF THE SEA

Ariel looked lovingly at the man she had rescued. Although her father forbade her to swim to the surface, the adventurous mermaid couldn't help her desire to be a part of the human world. As Prince Eric lay unconscious, she touched his face tenderly. He was so handsome!

She wished with all her heart that she could remain on this beach and dance with this man of her dreams. "What would I give to stay here beside you?" she sang. "What would I do to see you smiling at me?" Somehow, she was determined to find a way!

Sebastian, her father's trusted friend, anxiously tried to persuade Ariel that she would be happier under the sea. King Triton wanted him to keep an eye on his  youngest daughter, and Sebastian did not want to disappoint the sea king. "Down here is your home," he told Ariel, but despite his efforts to make her understand the wonders of the ocean, nothing could change her wish to be with Prince Eric. She was in love.

Only Flounder, her best friend, understood. Finding a statue of the Prince that had gone down with the shipwreck, he surprised Ariel.

"Flounder, you're the best!" she cried. "It looks just like him."

As she was imagining a romance with Eric, King Triton appeared in Ariel's secret grotto. Seeing

her collection of things from the "barbarian" world above,

he raised his trident and destroyed all of Ariel's treasures in

a final attempt to protect her from the dangers of the

human world.

Upset, Ariel sought the help of the Sea Witch, Ursula. In exchange for the mermaid's voice, Ursula transformed her tail into legs. She would remain human only if she received a kiss of true love before the sun set on the third day.

Happy to be human at last, Ariel wiggled her toes

excitedly while Sebastian watched in shock. "I'm going to march myself home right now and tell the sea king," he said, but when he looked at the sadness in Ariel's eyes he knew that she would never be happy as a mermaid. "All right," he decided. "I'll help you find your prince."

Scuttle, Ariel's seagull friend, excitedly arranged a dress. It wasn't long before Prince Eric arrived.

"You're the one!" he exclaimed. "The one I have been looking for!" Ariel nodded, but she couldn't talk. Eric remembered that the girl who had rescued him had the most beautiful voice. "Oh, you couldn't be who I thought," he sighed.

Still, he helped her to the castle, and when they ate

dinner together that night, Ariel made him laugh for the

first time in weeks. The next day he took her on a tour of

his kingdom, enchanted by her enthusiasm for everything

from horses to

puppet shows. She

pulled him eagerly

into a dance, and

she was thrilled

when he let her

take the reins on

the ride back to the

castle. Impressed and surprised by her fun-loving nature,

Eric thoroughly enjoyed his new guest.

Sebastian decided to create a romantic mood that

evening as Ariel and Eric rowed together in a quiet

lagoon. With soft music and moonlight on the water, the

Prince found himself leaning to kiss Ariel.

Suddenly, Ursula's pet eels tipped the boat!

Hypnotizing Eric, the Sea Witch transformed herself into

the beautiful Vanessa. Pretending to be his mysterious dream girl, she arranged a wedding to make sure that Ariel's plan for love would fail.

Scuttle gathered creatures of the ocean to help him stall

the wedding while Flounder pulled Ariel to the ship. As her friends tugged a magic necklace from Vanessa's neck, Ariel's voice was restored and the spell on Prince Eric was broken. He ran to his true love, relieved that she had been the girl he wanted all along. But their kiss was too late. Ariel had

become a mermaid once again, and Ursula pulled her into the water.

"I lost her once. I'm not going to lose her again!" yelled the Prince as he dived into the depths of the ocean. Using strength, and the power of true love, Eric destroyed the powerful Sea Witch.

As he lay exhausted on the shore, Ariel watched him from afar.

Turning to Sebastian, King Triton asked, "She really does love him, doesn't she?" With tenderness, he granted his beautiful daughter her greatest wish. As Ariel married

her prince, she finally knew true happiness. Sebastian, Flounder and Scuttle applauded with all of the creatures of the sea as Eric kissed his bride under a rainbow coloured with joy.

Disney's

TARZAN ®

You'll Always Be in My Heart

Young Tarzan looked with anguish at his reflection in the water and covered his face with mud. He desperately wanted to fit in with the other gorillas. "Why am I different?" he thought. He wanted to look like the rest of his family. He wanted to move as surely through

the trees and be as strong, too.

When his mother, Kala, found him, she felt his pain. Trying to comfort Tarzan, she showed him that they had the same hands and that her heartbeat was the same as his. Enveloped in his mother's hug, the boy felt a new strength and determination. "I'll be the best ape ever!" he promised.

True to his word, Tarzan grew into an adult with great

skills. He imitated the jungle animals and wrestled with his best friend, Terk, until he developed ways to overcome her superior strength. He swung from trees with great speed. With a spear he had invented, he was even able to rescue Kerchak, the gorilla leader, from the vicious leopard, Sabor.

Proudly, he earned acceptance from his peers. Up until the day he met Jane, Tarzan had put his doubts and miseries behind him.

When gunshots rang out one day, Tarzan investigated the strange noise. He was surprised to come upon three strange creatures. Clayton, a hunter, was leading Professor Porter and his daughter, Jane, on an expedition to study gorillas.

When Jane stayed behind to sketch a young baboon, Tarzan rescued her from the baboon's angry family. After the terrifying chase, Jane tried to back away from the wild man, but he came closer to her, touching her hands with a look of fascination. They were just like his! When he listened to her heartbeat and laid her head against his

own chest, she was afraid, but she realized that he wasn't going to hurt her. Though his eyes were intense, his smile was kind and his manner gentle.

"Tarzan," he spoke, pointing to himself, and they began to communicate. Slowly, Tarzan learned Jane's language. Visiting the human camp, he was fascinated with pictures of people and places. Everything was new to Tarzan. Jane and her father, excited by his enthusiasm, became Tarzan's teachers.

"I've never seen him so happy," Tantor said to Terk as the friends watched Tarzan pick flowers for Jane. He could not stop thinking about her. The bond between them had become more than a simple attraction. One morning, Tarzan arrived at the campsite but was surprised to learn that it was time for Jane to leave.

"Jane. Stay!" pleaded Tarzan as he handed her the

flowers. Crying, Jane ran away. She was as upset as Tarzan about her leaving.

Nearby, Clayton was forming a wicked plan. Wanting to capture the gorillas, he made Tarzan believe that Jane might stay if she could meet the apes.

Jane and her father were thrilled when Tarzan brought them to his family. Joyfully, Jane watched Tarzan talking to the young gorillas. "Can you teach me?" Jane asked.

Gently, Tarzan helped her form the gorilla words. As the apes reacted noisily, Jane wanted to know what he had taught her to say. "Jane stays with Tarzan," he told her, but she shook her head.

That evening Tarzan sat in a tree watching the distant boat anchored offshore. He wasn't sure what he should

do. Kala had told him he was her son, but he looked like the humans. Where did he belong?

Then his mother found him. Silently she led him to
the tree house where she had found him years ago.
An old picture of his human family was still on the floor.
"I just want you to be happy . . . whatever you decide,"
she told him.

Moments later, he had dressed in his father's clothes. "No matter where I go you will always be my mother," said Tarzan as he headed towards the beach. "And you will always be in my heart," she replied.

Sadly, Tantor

and Terk watched the dinghy pull away. "We didn't even get to say goodbye," said the elephant regretfully. Then a wild cry of despair reached shore. Tarzan was in trouble!

Quickly Tantor and Terk swam to the ship where Clayton had locked their friend in the hold. Bravely fighting off thugs, they released

Tarzan and Jane. "I thought I was never going to see you again!" sobbed Terk.

Calling the jungle animals for help, they battled Clayton and his men, but Kerchak was shot trying to save

Tarzan. "Forgive me for not understanding that you have always been one of us," the dying gorilla told Tarzan. "Take care of our family . . . my son."

Even though she had said a tearful goodbye to Tarzan, once Jane was on the boat she realized that she loved him too much to leave. Splashing back to shore, she embraced him joyfully, as friends and family cheered. "Oo-oo-ee-eh-ou," said Jane. "Jane stays with Tarzan!"

MULAN

FRIENDLY ADVICE

Long ago, and far beyond the Great Wall of China, a tiny dragon named Mushu left his ancestral home in search of a young girl, Mulan. Mulan had cut her hair and dressed as a man to take her father's place in the war

against the fierce
Huns. Mushu was
supposed to protect
and guard her.

"Walk like a
man. Legs apart,"
advised Mushu, as
she entered camp.
"Punch guys in the
arm, they like that
stuff. Call them names and spit a lot."

Every time Mushu gave her advice, Mulan caused

more trouble. Soon all of the new recruits were fighting. The camp was in total chaos when Captain Shang arrived.

"My name is . . . uh . . . Ping," Mulan told Shang, as she awkwardly tried to sound like a man.

Recently promoted, Shang was wary of possible troublemakers.

Shang was a strong and skilful leader, and although Mulan

felt clumsy and inadequate, she worked hard and used her mind to finally win his respect. All of the soldiers admired Ping's determination and they were inspired by her actions. Still, not even her best friends,

Chien-Po, Ling and Yao, knew that "Ping" was a woman.

Shang led his troop swiftly to join the Imperial Army.

Mulan and her friends sang songs. Sadly, their good cheer

came to a halt when they discovered that the army and the

village lay in ruins. Shang was especially upset when he realized that his father, the General, had been killed in battle. As Mulan tried to comfort him, the Huns returned.

Proving to be a great and courageous soldier, Mulan, with Mushu's help, caused an avalanche that buried the enemy. Wounded in battle, Mulan was still able to jump on her horse and pull Shang from the onrushing snow.

As Chien-Po and the others helped them to safety, Shang regained consciousness and looked at Mulan with admiration. "From now on you have my trust," Shang said, thanking her. Mulan's smile soon turned to pain,

and as her wound was treated, they all learned the truth about "Ping".

At this time in China, Mulan's deception was punishable by death, but Shang spared her. "A life for a life," he declared.

Dejected, Mulan watched the troops march away, leaving her alone with Mushu. With a heavy heart Mulan confided in her friend: "I just wanted to do things right, so that when I looked in the mirror I would see someone worthwhile. But I was wrong. I see nothing."

Trying to make her feel better, Mushu confessed that he had set out to

make Mulan a hero so that he would regain his position as guardian. "At least you risked your life to help people you love. I risked your life to help myself," he told her. Mulan embraced the little dragon. How could she be angry with such a friend?

This quiet moment was shattered as Mulan realized that a few of the Huns had survived. Racing to the Imperial City to

warn Shang, Mulan
arrived moments before
the Emperor was taken
prisoner.

Chien-Po, Ling and
Yao tried unsuccessfully
to break down the palace
door. "Hey, guys, I have
an idea!" Mulan called.
Eager for the help of their
quick-thinking friend,
they let Mulan dress them

as women. Together they scaled the wall and attacked the unsuspecting Huns. Realizing that he could trust her, Shang soon followed her lead.

They rescued the Emperor, but Shan Yu, the Hun leader, angrily attacked Shang. To protect him, Mulan revealed herself as the soldier who had defeated him at the mountain. With ferocity, Shan Yu began to chase her. Putting their heads

together, the girl and the dragon hatched a plan. Leading

Shan Yu to the top of the palace, Mulan grabbed his

sword and pinned his cloak to the roof just as Mushu

shot a rocket towards him. Shan Yu was blasted into a tower of fireworks.

Mulan was happy to leave for home. She realized that she was special enough as herself, and that she had friends she could count on. She presented the Emperor's sword to her father, and he welcomed her back. Shang followed her, realizing, with the Emperor's help, that his feelings for Mulan had grown. She was much more than a good fighter. Finally, Mulan's heart was full.

As for Mushu, the joyful little dragon regained his guardianship. "Send out for eggrolls!" he shouted to the happy Ancestors.

LION KING

Love Withstands Anything

Kiara was warned never to go to the Outlands, but her father wouldn't tell her why. "What could be so terrible?" Kiara wondered curiously. As soon as her faithful guardians, Timon and Pumbaa, were distracted by

their favourite pastime of eating bugs, she crept away and ventured to the forbidden land.

There she met another lion cub. The two cubs helped each other cross a dangerous river full of crocodiles. Exhilarated by the adventure, Kiara exclaimed, "We make a good team!" With admiration she smiled at Kovu. "You were really brave," she told him.

He looked at her curiously. His mother, Zira, had always taught him that Pride

Landers couldn't be trusted, yet this lioness had saved him from the crocodile's teeth at least once.

"Yeah, you were pretty brave, too," Kovu admitted.

Happily, Kiara began to prance around him. She was laughing and wanted to play, but Kovu didn't understand.

 He had never played tag. Just as Kiara began to make him smile and laugh, their parents arrived with bared teeth!

Kiara's father, Simba, was an enemy of Kovu's mother.

Because Zira was loyal to Scar, who had murdered

Simba's father, the Lion King had banished her to the

Outlands. Focused on revenge, she was raising Kovu to

hate. Her plan was to overthrow Simba and make her son the new King.

"Take your cub and get out!" Simba ordered. As Kovu and Kiara were separated, the friends sadly whispered

goodbye.

It was not until they were fully grown that the two saw each other again. Kiara

was a beautiful young lioness out on her first hunt. She had made her father promise not to interfere, but Simba was protective of his only daughter. As usual, he sent Timon and Pumbaa to watch over her . . . from a distance.

When Kiara came upon Timon and Pumbaa during her chase, she felt betrayed and angry.

Wanting to prove that she could manage on her own, she raced away to hunt in the Outlands. Unaware that the Outsiders were watching her every move, she fell into their trap easily.

Quickly Zira and her followers set the plains on fire, surrounding Kiara. The young lioness ran until she fell unconscious. It was then that Kovu appeared. Trained to avenge Scar, he rescued the Princess only to get closer to his goal of killing Simba. He was ready for anything . . . except falling in love.

"Thanks for saving me," Kiara said after Simba reluctantly allowed Kovu to return with her to Pride Rock. She was happy to have him back in her life and she unwittingly distracted Kovu from his mission. Leading him away from her father, Kiara asked him to impress her with his expertise in stalking.

As Kovu showed her how to pounce quietly, they ran into Timon and Pumbaa. The silly animals were trying to rid their feeding ground

of pesky birds. "Lend a voice?" asked Timon. With a roar, Kiara gave chase.

"Why are we doing this?" asked Kovu, puzzled. "For fun!" answered Kiara. She showed Kovu the joy of laughter, and he was exhilarated by the new experience.

Even after being chased by angry hippos he was happier than he had ever been. "What a blast!" he shouted, smiling at Kiara. By accident, the two bumped noses bashfully. "You're okay, kid!" said Timon.

That night Kovu and Kiara lay on the grass looking at the stars. "Do you think Scar's up there?" Kovu asked tentatively. "He wasn't my father, but he is a part of me."

Kiara knew he was troubled and tried to comfort her friend, but he pulled away. Confused, Kovu wasn't sure if he

should follow his mother's plan or follow his heart.

Nearby, the wise baboon, Rafiki, was watching. Leading the two lions to a place he called Upendi, Rafiki placed them in a boat. As Kovu watched Kiara during the wild ride, he gave in to his feelings for her. Kissing and laughing, Kiara guessed, "Upendi means love, doesn't it?"

Deciding not to follow in Scar's footsteps, Kovu made peace with Simba. But unawares, he and Simba were ambushed by the Outsiders. "No!" yelled Kovu, but it was too late. Simba believed he was responsible for the setup, and he exiled Kovu.

Heartbroken, Kiara knew that Kovu couldn't have been responsible for the ambush. Running away, she joined Kovu in the ashes of the fire.

"Hey, look! We are one," Kovu said looking at their reflection together in the water. As the wind blew the ashes away to reveal grass underneath, they knew their love could survive anything. Racing back to the Pride Lands, Kiara put an end to the war. "We are one!" she declared.

With peace settling over Pride Rock once more, Simba accepted Kovu's relationship with Kiara. Together, they joined the King and Queen for a celebration of unity.

The End